LOVE,

GHOSTS, & facial hair

LOVE,

GHOSTS, & facial hair

steven herrick

Simon Pulse
New York London Toronto Sydney

**Dedicated to the backyard cricket
pitch at Katoomba.**

First Simon Pulse edition March 2004

Copyright © 1996 by Steven Herrick
Published by arrangement with University of Queensland Press
Originally published in Australia in 1996 as *Love, Ghosts and Nose Hair* by University of Queensland Press

SIMON PULSE
An imprint of Simon & Schuster
Children's Publishing Division
1230 Avenue of the Americas
New York, NY 10020

Printed in the United States of America

10 9 8 7 6 5 4 3 2 1

Library of Congress Control Number 2003110835

ISBN 0-689-86710-7 (Simon Pulse pbk.)

CONTENTS

my family

1   My name   *2*
2   My family (the dream one)   *4*
3   My family (the real one)   *5*
4   My family (the truth)   *6*
5   Sex, sport, & nose hair   *8*
6   Desiree on sex   *10*
7   Another poem on sex, sport, & nose hair   *11*
8   A writer   *12*
9   The great poem   *14*
10   Love is like a gobstopper   *15*
11   Desiree on facial hair   *16*
12   Violence in the family   *17*

there's a ghost in our house

13   Cancer   *20*
14   Don't believe   *21*
15   The photo   *22*
16   The family holiday   *23*
17   There's a ghost in our house   *24*
18   Shoes, socks, the lock on the bathroom door   *26*
19   Coooeee   *28*
20   Dad writes poetry   *30*
21   The family team   *32*

22 The cubbyhouse   *34*
23 Wine   *36*
24 Signature   *37*
25 Katoomba   *38*
26 The new teacher   *40*
27 Shiver   *42*

the wild orchard

28 Valentine's day   *46*
29 Annabel on Jack   *47*
30 I kiss Annabel's photo   *48*
31 There's more to life than Annabel   *50*
32 First date   *52*
33 Annabel writes poetry!   *54*
34 Annabel   *55*
35 Annabel and the ghost   *56*
36 The ghost is away   *58*
37 The fireplace   *60*
38 Ezra finds the hut   *61*
39 Megalong creek hut   *62*
40 Annabel and the wild orchard   *63*

making a living

41 The funeral   *66*
42 Desiree   *67*
43 Careers   *68*
44 Selling up   *70*
45 The wreck   *71*
46 Dad didn't come home last night   *72*
47 Sunday lunch   *74*
48 The earthquake   *76*

49   What I do for a living   *78*
50   All her brain cells   *79*
51   Solo Desiree   *80*
52   The ghost spoke to me last night   *82*
53   Father of the year   *83*
54   Annabel writes a poem for english   *85*
55   Winter Annabel   *87*

echoes

56   My son is seeing a girl   *90*
57   Sex, sport, and nose hair (according to
        Annabel)   *92*
58   Blue mountains school   *94*
59   Bloody rain   *96*
60   Confessions   *98*
61   The right reasons   *100*
62   The bike ride   *102*
63   Monday, the last before holidays   *104*
64   Ms Curling   *106*
65   Annabel kisses   *108*
66   It's easy   *109*
67   37 lines   *110*
68   Telling the ghost   *112*
69   Echoes   *114*

My Family

My name

My name is Jack
not Jackson
or Jackie
not Jack-in-the-box
    laughing like an echo
not hit the road Jack
not Jack the rat
or Jack, go wash your face
or Jack rabbit
    lifting my head to get shot
or Jacqueline
not Jack of all trades
    master of none
or car Jack
or Jack Frost
not Jackpot
    the name of a loser

or Jackboot
or Jacktar
or Jackknife
or Jacket
     something to wrap yourself in
not just Jack
or Jack of hearts
but
JACK

OK?

My family (the dream one)

There's my Dad
dressed in his best blue suit
counting his money ($10,000, $11,000, $12,000 ...)
My Mum
she'll be home soon
she's starring in another movie
so she's acting late.
And my sister? she's away.
She's a Nun, helping the poor in Africa
they had her on *60 Minutes* last week
Saint Sister they call her.
My brother?
he's outside polishing his Porsche.
And me
I'm just starting my maths homework.
I love maths.

My family (the real one)

There's my Dad
snoring in his chair, still in his work clothes
sleeping without a shower for the third day running.
My Mum
she's wearing those pink curlers in her hair
looks like a Space Cadet to me.
And my sister's in the bathroom
she's dyeing her hair orange
I think it'll suit her.
My brother?
he's in jail, we expect him home next year.
And I'm here writing this, watching the footy on TV
and doing everything possible to avoid
homework.

My family (the truth)

Actually, truth be known
they're both wrong.
I live with my Dad
and my sister.
My Dad works at a newspaper
he says he tells "edited lies" all day
he's a journalist
which means I never see him.
He leaves home at 7am
and returns at night
smelling of cigarette smoke and defeat.
He walks in
reheats the dinner
and asks me if I've done my homework.
He's OK though.
He talks to me on the weekends
and that's enough for a parent.
My sister I like!
yeah I know
you're not supposed to like your sister
but Desiree's great.

She left school last year
went right out and got a job.
She's Assistant Manager of a bookshop.
She says they'll stock my first book
when it's published.
She's nineteen.
Tall, dark eyes, long black hair,
and
this faint trace of soft light hair on her top lip!
that's what I like about her
she's upfront
other girls might wax it
but not Des
I tell her it looks sexy
and I think it does (for my sister!)
so Des & me
get on fine
she even talks to me
about Ms Curling
and Annabel Browning.

Sex, sport, & nose hair

I'm a normal guy.
An average sixteen-year-old.
I think about sex, sport, & nose hair.
Sex mostly.
How to do it
how to get someone to do it with me
who I should ask for advice.
My friends are useless
they know nothing.
We sit, at lunchtime,
trying to make sense of that
impenetrable mystery called girls.
I've thought of asking Ms Curling
she's the type who'd look me in the eye
and talk straight
but I could never hold her stare
I'd start dribbling, or blushing, or coughing
or worse

I'd get an erection!
they happen at the worst times.
In the bus
In Science class
I spent all Friday night thinking I must be
perverted to get excited during Science!
so, I can't ask my teachers, or friends,
Dad?
it's so long since he had sex
he'd have trouble remembering.
I'd be better asking him
about nose hair!

Desiree!
She'll tell me ...

*D*esiree on sex

"Des, I want to know about sex."

    "Like what?"

"Like how, why, when, & who with."

    "How is simple. Hands, lips
    kissing, touching.
    Why? Because it feels good
    and costs nothing, except
    for the condom.
    When? When Dad's not home.
    Or on the weekend, somewhere nice,
    like the hut near Megalong Creek.
    Who with? Can't help you, sorry.
    Why not ask Annabel Browning on a date?
    You keep talking about her ..."

Trust Desiree to answer
everything about sex in about fifty words
and bring up Annabel Browning.

Another poem on sex, sport, & nose hair

Sex is late-night games on the computer
    thinking "there must be better things to do".
Sex is the morning newspaper crimes
    with my Dad shaking his head
    saying "what a world, what a world".
Sex is with a condom
    or so the school counsellor says.
Sex is the beach in summer
    the smell of suntan oil
    the long train ride home, alone,
    reading a book.
Sex is acne, greasy hair, and shopping
    for the Hollywood gloss of magazines
    and movies.
Sport is as much energy as sex
    yet half the fun, I imagine.
Sport is the only time
    you'd get me wrapping my arms
    around Peter Blake's legs!
Sport is the way we decide who should
    be the School Captain.
Sport is money, broken noses, & played
    by guys with thick necks!
Nose hair is my destiny.
Nose hair will prevent me from having sex
    until I'm too old to care.
Nose hair is the first thing I check in the morning.
Nose hair bristles in the afternoon wind.
Nose hair keeps my mind off girls, maths,
    and the adventure of sleeping.

A writer

I'm going to be a writer
I decided yesterday
while Ms Curling, my Art teacher,
had my head cradled in her arms,
wiping my brow
with a warm towel.
We were surrounded by
twenty-one fellow students, all in football gear,
and two less-concerned teachers.
It seems my face and someone's elbow
had a close encounter.
the result, Ms Curling's *Chanel #5*
wafting through
my newly-broken nose.
Maybe it was this,
and her concerned caress,
or the thought
of another fifteen games
left in the season
that decided it ...

yes
I'm going to be a writer
beat the typewriter
not my mates
no more change-room jokes on muscles
or competitions for the smelliest socks.
I'm retiring
joining the guys on the outer.
I'm going to wear dark clothes
and an intense expression.

If nothing else
I hope it will attract the girls.

The great poem

I have just written a great poem.
A Classic.
One that's so good
University Professors will read it, badly,
in front of hundreds of students
twenty years
        after I die
to prove to the world
what a jewel
what a gift
what a gem
        I gave
what a poet I was.
Here in my Blue Mountains garret
I light another imaginary cigarette
        to celebrate
death and the poem.
I'm sending it to every publisher in the land
I want them to fight for it
I'm sitting at my desk trying to choose the pen
I'll use to sign the contracts
        to sign the Movie Rights
I'm sorry it's night, or I'd ring the Chat Shows
to arrange to read it live to the Nation!
Ms Curling, my Dad, Desiree
will shake their heads in disbelief.
    A great poem from "what's his name" …

*L**ove is like a gobstopper*

Love is like a gobstopper
it's true
you spend all your childhood
wanting that perfect round life-giving
never-ending ball of sweetness
you look through the shop window
    your mouth waters
    legs shake
    eyes go in and out of focus
until that desired gobstopper is yours.
    You hold it
    cherish it
    kiss it
    dream about it
sleep with it under your pillow
wake up sticky
and hope you'll never be alone
but like all lovers
you want more
so one tempting night
you close your eyes
push it all the way into your mouth
and taste its wonder
    then you swallow it
    choke
    and die!
Love is like a gobstopper.

*D*esiree *on facial hair*

It's Jack who's to blame
his obsession with facial hair
has got me looking at my moustache
God! he's even got me calling it that
when it's only light lip hair
and now I can't look at anyone
without noticing the shadow above their mouth.
Three weeks of research has proven
that every woman I know has facial hair.
The only people without it seem to be
models and movie stars
and we all know about their grip on reality!
so I'm keeping mine
despite my hairdresser
mentioning it every time I see her.
Waxing, electrolysis, dyeing —
give me a break.
And besides, I'm beginning to like it
maybe Jack is right
maybe it is sexy
let's face it
it's certainly more attractive than nose hair.

Violence in the Family

Today I'm going to watch my Dad
    hit a white ball with a big silver stick
when he's hit the ball
he's going to walk after it
    carrying a whole bag of big sticks
when he finds the ball, hiding, grass-stained
he's going to hit it again
    until it does what it's told
    and falls in the hole.
Sometimes it refuses
    and he bashes the big stick
    on the ground in threat
occasionally he drowns the ball in a lake
    and walks silently away
once he stamped his petulant feet
    quickly looked around
    alone, and ashamed
    and gave the little ball an almighty smack.
After doing this for a few hours
    he'll put the ball and sticks in the car
    drive home
    and boast about his game to me and Des.
One day he asked Desiree to join him
    but she smiled no
    as she took a knife from the drawer
    went to the fridge
    dragged an onion out
    and slowly, deliberately
    cut its head off.

There's a Ghost in Our House

Cancer

They said it was a harmless lump
    it wasn't
they said the signs were good
    they weren't
they said she needed tests
    we all did
they said they found it too late
    no, too early
they said she had six months
    she didn't
they said the pills eased the pain
    they only gave them to Mum
they said Dad was being strong
    he wasn't
they said Desiree and I didn't understand
    we did
they said it was hereditary
    now Dad calls the doctor if I get a headache
they said the hospital room smelt fresh
    it smelt of death
they said the funeral was stirring
we came home alone.

*D*on't believe

Don't believe in leaders
don't believe anyone who calls you mate
　　twice in one sentence
don't believe in people who always do what's right
don't believe in people with religious placards
　　who stop you in the street and say
　　"this will only take five minutes of your time"
don't believe in tax cuts
don't believe anyone who parts their hair in the middle
don't believe what you read, unless I wrote it
don't believe stallholders at community markets
　　who say "yes, of course it's handcrafted"
don't believe school counsellors
　　who say they can help you
don't believe in money, unless you've got some
don't believe in pop stars with runny noses
don't believe pop stars anyway
don't believe teachers
　　they really want to dress like that
don't believe anyone who votes Liberal
don't believe anyone who votes National
　　BELIEVE anyone who votes Labor
　　no one that stupid could lie
don't believe anyone who owns a Barry Manilow CD
don't believe anyone who owns a Guns & Roses CD
to be safe, don't believe anyone who owns a CD player
and never, but never, believe doctors who say
"everything will be all right".

The photo

It's the only photo I carry
the four of us
Dad with his arm around Mum's waist
both standing in the holiday fresh water
Desiree and me pushing into the frame
I'm pointing at Dad's arm
I'd never seen them stand that close
Desiree is looking straight at the camera
     her chest out
       the pride of a one-piece swimsuit
       at thirteen, sunning in the attention.

After the photo Mum and Dad
     lie on the sand
     they hold hands
I keep kicking the ball their way
     like a troublesome dog with a stick
     no one wants to throw.
Desiree is off talking to boys
I kick the ball for the return of the waves
and count how many times Mum and Dad kiss.

Seven years ago
on the beach
Mum and Dad
kissed
twenty-four times
and never once
saw anyone else
or thought of anyone else.

Twenty-four times.

It's the only photo I carry
it's in my wallet.

The family holiday

I remember that last holiday with my wife,
Jack and Desiree.
Fish and chips, with no dishes to wash
teaching Jack to bodysurf
sand in our shorts
Desiree talking to the boys at the shops
        looking to see if we could hear
ice-cream for dessert
kissing my wife on the beach
the orange evening sky
walking from headland to lighthouse
Jack kicking the ball at seagulls
the rain that only fell at night
        and cleared to summer at six am.
The distant hum of Saturday sport
everyone nodding "hello" down the main street
Desiree and Jack sleeping till late
my wife, my wife
talking to me
        and I'm drinking it in.

There's a ghost in our house

There's a ghost in our house
in a red evening dress
black stockings
    and Mum's slingback shoes
her hair whispers
    over white shoulders
as she dances through the rooms.
In Desiree's
    she cleans under the bed
folds the five pairs of Levi's
Des wears for months without washing.
In my room
    she flips through my poems
to the one about Mum & Dad at the beach
    the poem glows as I sleep.
In Dad's room
    she sits at the dresser
I can see her
    smiling at the mirror too scared
to announce her presence.

Once, when I stood to watch
     she winked
like an over-excited schoolgirl
     the ghost winked at me.
Annabel Browning
Ms Curling
and whatever future I'd planned
disappeared
in that moment of me and the ghost
     playing hide & seek
breathing
     in the shadow of history
retying a cord
     that should never have been cut.

There's a ghost in our house
in Mum's
red evening dress.

Shoes, socks, the lock on the bathroom door

When I think of our house
I think of shoes
socks
and the lock on the bathroom door.
Dad's golf shoes on the washing machine
Desiree's work shoes on her wardrobe
her Baxter boots flung over the lounge
    with the rest of her attached.
Dad's socks, as he walks to the bathroom
Dad's socks, soaking in the sink
Desiree's stockings hanging from the shower rail
    the run in her black ones.
My football boots, shiny, worn once
    in the garbage
my Doc's with the toe pushing through
Dad's brown shoes
    "brown shoes, brown personality" Desiree says.
Desiree's baby booties tied to her mirror
    pink, with pink bows, my Mum's handiwork.
My socks, the ones with Batman on them
    Dad's idea of cool!
my football socks, full of spare change
    sagging from a hook on the wall.

The lock on the bathroom door
    when my Dad reads the paper.
    Desiree every morning in a rush.
    Me, when I eat too much
    or when I want to write and the TV's on
where I'm sitting now
in the bath, writing this,
thinking one day, to please Dad
I'm going to have to wear
those bloody Batman socks!

*C*oooeee

Me and Dad
have nothing to do this Saturday
so we go for a walk
through the bush
to our favourite spot
"Jack's Lookout"
Dad named it
on our first visit
with Mum and Desiree
when I was five.
It's a granite rock
high above Megalong Valley
and on a sunny day
you can see forever.

I loved it there
the parrots chimed through the gums
a stream rippled below
and I think of our first visit
the picnic lunch
and Dad, hands cupped, shouting
"Coooooeeeee"
across the cliffs
their echo sounding once each
for the four of us.

At five years old, I thought Dad
was shouting
"do a wee"
and kept asking him
for one more echo
A grown man telling the world
about his toilet habits
and his kids rolling on the rock
saying
"One more Dad, one more"
and him, never understanding
why we laughed the whole weekend.

I'm sixteen now,
I'm trying to decide
as we walk this bush track
whether to ask my Dad
to shout once more
and tell him about it
or keep a secret
between Des, and Mum, and me,
and the family history.

*D*ad writes poetry

Jack, when I was sixteen
I wanted to play football every day
until I was old, thirty-five, or forty.
And at forty
I wanted to buy a house on a cliff
wander to the beach
make love in the sand
then come home and drink all afternoon.
This seemed a good plan for my life.
My teacher said I was being unrealistic
my Mother said I was being stupid
my Dad said I wasn't that good at football
and my girlfriend didn't say anything
        because I didn't have one.
So at sixteen
I set off on my plan.
The first game of football
        I broke my arm
the first time at the beach
        I nearly drowned
the first time I drank lots of beer
        I puked
and the first time I made love
        I'd rather not say.
So I gave up football
        and swimming

although I still occasionally practise drinking
and alone at fifty
     making love is not such an issue
     although everyone says it should be.
So Jack, when I look back
the only thing that was worthwhile,
apart from having you and Desiree
and falling in love with your Mum,
     was writing poetry.
At sixteen I thought poems were for old people
and always about flowers, or death,
or "ducks gliding gracefully across the millpond"
but the only ducks I saw
     were in Chinese take-away shops
so I guess I have learnt something
     even if it's taken me
                    half my life.

The family team

We wanted more children
I planned a football team
Desiree's kick in your Mother's stomach
        held promise
        a backyard of winners
we had a long list of names
        ready, in the top drawer
we saved your baby clothes
we planned extra bedrooms
we promised your Grandma
        (she held on for years)
we had dreams of a farm
we'd welcome each year with a child
we'd fill the one-teacher-school with our own
I was going to learn to milk a cow
                        drive a tractor
                        change a nappy
                        all at the same time!
we would never grow old
        with so many children

but the cancer ripped our family
and this heart
        that now only pumps blood

we wanted more children
we would never grow old
now
I want more children
and your Mother will never grow old.

The cubbyhouse

Dad's thinking of knocking down the cubbyhouse.
It sits, weed lonely at the bottom of the yard
home of rusted toys
    rain-soaked curtains
and my initials carved inside the door.
Dad says he could use the space
    and the wood.
The last time any of us went inside
was the night Des and I got locked out
and needed somewhere to wait.

So Dad and I
    hammer, saw, crowbar,
circle the cubbyhouse
    neither wanting to swing the first blow
and I check inside for my initials
and show Dad
and he fingers the hinge of the door
and smells the scent of old timber
and gets that faraway look in his eyes
as he tells me how
    he built this
the day of the 1986 Grand Final
    Dad in the backyard hammering nails
    as Parramatta hammered Canterbury

and he tells me that
Des and I climbed in
as soon as the floor was up
and we didn't leave till dark
and every night for two weeks
Mum had to bring dinner down here
and once, in summer,
Des and I, and Dad,
slept here all night
        and told stories to the wind.

Dad and I pick up the tools
and put them back in the shed.
Dad takes one look at the untouched cubby
and says he's heading into town
to the hardware
        for some paint.

Wine

He drinks red wine during the week
one glass at dinner
another for dessert
    he pats his stomach
    smiles, with perfect teeth
and tells us
    he's fighting ulcers and a heart condition
    the best way he knows.
Desiree says
    at least red wine doesn't smell,
    not like the bottle of Riesling
    he drinks for Saturday lunch
and afterwards
    he tries to interest me
    in a game of cricket.
At sixteen years of age
    I realise how regular
    adults need humouring
Desiree tells him to act his age
Dad and I ignore her
    as I tap the cricket bat
    in front of the stumps
and Dad walks back to his mark
    a glass in one hand
    ball in the other
and for the past five years
I've watched him bowl his gangly
leg-spin
and never once
    spill a drop.

*S*ignature

Ezra is my friend
he's finishing school soon
    moving straight to work
    and his father's designs.
I'll miss him
we sit against the fence
he takes a poem he's written
    out of the sling for his broken arm
I read it
    his parents arguing down the page.
Ezra looks across the oval
tapping his fingers
on the plaster cast
I can see the poem hurt more than the arm
he's waiting for me
    to lie
    or tear it up
    or tell him to change the last line.
And I can't help thinking
that the poem and the arm
happened in the same place
and which came first
which will last longer
and then I know what to do
    I give him back the poem
    smile
and ask if I can sign my name
on his plaster cast.

K atoomba

This is the only school assignment I've enjoyed.
I've been looking through a book of
Aboriginal Place Names
for a study of our suburb
whose name means
"place where waters tumble over hill"
now this may have been accurate before 1813
but today I'd say it's either
"place where Japanese tourists tumble over hill"
or
"place where polluted water stagnates".
If I had a choice I'd call it
Cobba-da-mana
meaning "caught by the head"
and I know a few Year 9s that name suits perfectly.
Or this one, in honour of our
Physical Education teacher:
Barnawather ... "deaf and dumb"
or Desiree's favourite:
Pugonda, meaning "fight".
I love the way you can spit these words out.
I'm glad I come from Katoomba
not "Kensington Gardens" or "Pacific Vista".
Maybe we can also change the names of our States?
For Victoria (named after some dead Queen)
give me Pullabooka

for Tasmania — Murrumba
South Australia — Kameruka
New South Wales — Cudgewa
for Queensland — Bulla Bulla
and for Western Australia how about
"People who play stupid football!"
no, OK, how about Wanbi,
meaning "wild dogs" —
I think that says it all.

The new teacher

He must teach Science
    see how he squints
    and looks at his lunch
    like a failed experiment.
Or Maths!
    the grey of his shorts
    the expanse of his ears
    the lovely floral tie & check shirt
    all add up.
He couldn't teach English
    because he's always reading
    and he seems able to string a few words together
    and, as yet,
    he hasn't misspelt his own name.
He's too old to teach History
    and the neat way he packs his briefcase
    implies a sense of place —
    maybe Geography?

No. Well, definitely not Physical Education
        because he doesn't have a moustache
        and he hasn't called anyone "mate" yet
so by class consensus
        we all agree on Industrial Arts
        the fine style of his wig
        gives it away —
that, and his spotless four-wheel drive
        with the "Eat beef, you bastards" sticker
we're sure he'll fit into this school
        like a burger into a bun.

_S_hiver

Sometimes in winter
when the mist buries our suburb
Desiree and I
walk to the golf course
(scene of Dad's weekend despair)
we crawl through the fence
and wander the fairways
    gleaming wet and dark
    in the chill evening.
We sit on the roof of the halfway hut.
I tell Desiree about my poems
    or school
    and try not to mention boys
    or else I'll set Des off!
Desiree talks about her work
    Dad, her clothes
    our house.
But tonight
with the mist closing down
    and dripping heavy from trees
Des tells me of talking to Mum
    just before she died
she tells me of
    the calm woman who held her hand
    and how her eyes never seemed to blink
    as she told Des

that we were the painkillers of her night
and she refused all regrets
in the time she had left
      to brush Desiree's hair back
and tell her what she felt
      the day the doctor diagnosed
and that day was the middle of a heatwave
      but she shivered
as she stepped from the surgery
and saw Dad waiting in the car
and both of us
      waving from the back seat.
But as we drove home
      Des and I told her of our school day
and she knew
      the doctor, the heatwave
      or this death
couldn't touch her
      not with Dad beside her
      and us in the back, talking.

I can feel Des crying beside me
I put my arm around her
we shiver together
      in the mist
and wait for it
      to clear.

The Wild Orchard

*V*alentine's day

Dear Annabel,

HAPPY VALENTINE'S DAY!
I wanted to give you this card in person,
but my sister told me that Valentine's Day wishes
must remain anomn, anunom, anonomus, nameless.
So, whoever you think I am is probably wrong.
But it's definitely not
Peter Blake, the school captain.
Let's face it, he couldn't even spell his own name,
let alone anonymous!
And it's not Alex Ricco, who seems to act louder
every time you walk past the gang at lunchtime.
Alex is busy right now writing a Valentine
to his basketball.
Anyway, think of nose hair!

Happy Valentine's
J   XXX

Annabel on Jack

He sent me a Valentine's card
    it took him six months to get this far
he almost signed it
he's as transparent as gladwrap
    but I like his smile
and the way he tries to meet my eyes
    and he doesn't play football
so he can't be too bad
    and unlike the rest of the school
he's not in love with baggy pants
    and baseball caps slapped on backwards
he doesn't say "Yo"
or call everyone "brother"
and act like he's from South-Central L.A.
I've never seen him in the company
    of a basketball
    or another girl
so if he gets the courage
    to ask me out
I'll say yes
    and worry about it
later.

I kiss Annabel's photo

I kiss Annabel's photo every night

it's an old voodoo trick
the ghost taught me

for years after Mum died
    I kissed her photo
other kids had teddy bears
    and tapes of Playschool
I cuddled a photo
I tucked myself in with a ghost
    and dreamed
    of holidays that lasted all summer
and parents holding hands
    and games where I always won
and the ghost walked to my room
    to push my hair back
    and smile love.

When Mum wasn't there
    and the holidays dried up
I ripped the photo from the album
and kissed it once every night
    until the ghost came.

So I kiss Annabel's photo
    and work my spell
just long enough to hope.

It can't do any harm
even if it won't do any good
    but you tell that
to the ghost and me.

There's more to life than Annabel

There's more to life than Annabel.
There's Science with Mr Edwards
    rattling his bones as he
    pours one chemical into another
    and on Monday morning
    twenty-eight students concentrate hard
    and hope for an explosion.
There's cold roast-beef sandwiches
    on white bread
    the canteen special on Monday
    and served till Friday.
There's lunchtime
    Ezra and me sitting on the fence
    hoping no-one asks us to join
    in basketball
    or football
    or putting long cold scratches in the duco
    of the Principal's new Volvo.
There's the books from the library
    and the last five I've read
    have been about aliens
    invading the world
    and two teenage heroes with computers
    and I swear I'm ripping up my library card.

There's more to life than Annabel
      but not this week
      when I've sent her a Valentine
      and right now
      I'm leaving Ezra on the fence
      as I see her walking across the oval
      and I'm asking her
      out
and was that a smile that creased her mouth …

*F*irst date

We're in the back seat
Annabel and me
    our knees are touching
    our elbows
    our legs
    our shoulders
I'm looking straight
    but I can see her
next to me on the bus
    our first date
witnessed by the early evening commuters
of the 482 Express to town.

The next three hours
    Annabel and I
will spend touching
    on the bus
    at the movies
    on the way home
I hope I can stay sane
    all night
not to say anything
    but say enough
not to do anything
    but do enough.

Desiree said
    "just be yourself"
Dad said
    "try to act better than you normally do"
while the ghost smiled all afternoon
    and beckoned me to reflect in the mirror.

I'd like to tell Annabel
    about the ghost
and Desiree's moustache
    and my poetry
but such secrets
    stay hidden
longer than a night on the bus.

Annabel turns and asks what I'm thinking
My Dad whispers
    "I'm thinking about the movie"
Desiree shouts
    "about you Annabel"
the ghost:
    "how nice it is to sit beside you"
as I gulp and ask
    "what do you think of facial hair on women?"
as the bus
    brakes sharply
  at the red light.

Annabel writes poetry

After the movie
　　which I can't remember
over coffee tasting of mud
　　with the banging of pinball machines
our hands 110 centimetres apart
　　on the shiny formica table
one hour left
　　to walk home
one hour
　　for me to say something
I blurt out the only word I shouldn't:
　　"poetry"

and Annabel's eyes,
　　dulled by cafe noise and smoke,
flash!
　　She writes poetry!
but not about her family
　　　　her friends
　　　　her future
she writes about bodies
　　　　their shape
　　　　the way they walk
the hinge of an arm around a waist
the machine rhythm of gymnastics
the bumping uglies that make brothers & sisters

and I forgot what we said
but we said enough

and I talked about the ghost
       without feeling foolish
and all the way home along Narrowneck Road
       the stars did their stuff
for Annabel and me
       and poetry!

Annabel

Look at her nose
                yes
look at her hair
                yes
at her vegetarian eyes
                yes yes yes

she is a cyclone
a calm
I float I spin
when I touch her arm.

Annabel and the ghost

I'm not scared
    or embarrassed
I'm excited
    he's telling me about the ghost
and I can see who she is
    and it makes perfect sense.
I remember being ten years old
and the stories my Mum
told me late at night
with the Southern Cross
tracking across my bedroom
and Mum making it part of each story
as she sat on the bed.
And Dad's snoring
with Mum whispering "Quiet, George,
you'll wake Annabel"
and how I tried hard not to giggle.
And the pancakes stacked
with strawberries and maple syrup
we'd have every Saturday breakfast
in fact, still have every Saturday
and for seven years I've reached
for a second helping
and winked at Mum.

And as Jack and I walk down Narrowneck Road
I look up at the Southern Cross
and think of Mum and Dad
sleeping now, Dad still snoring
and I think of Jack
at ten years old
alone
hugging a photo
and the ghost
makes complete and perfect sense.

*T*he ghost is away

The ghost didn't come home last night
I waited until dawn
excited
with the news of Annabel and me
I crept into Dad's room
and saw the empty mirror
the clothes in Desiree's room
remained unfolded
Desiree asleep in her Levi's
and the echo of the ghost
hung loose
I climbed out the window
and sat on the roof
one eye on the chimney
thinking of a ghost parading as Santa
the Southern Cross faded
as the sun crept up the mountain
and I called the ghost
and called again
and felt nine years old
waiting for Mum to come home
so I could tell her my day before I slept.

I climbed back through the window and into bed
and thought of Annabel
but she had the face of the ghost
and I must have dozed
as I woke sweating.
I looked at the calendar
seven years today
my Mum died
and now I know
why the ghost
is away.

The fireplace

Our house has a fireplace
one of those slow-combustion models
with the glass door
and the soot-black internal chimney.
My Dad cuts the Ironbark
with an axe he's had since he was a kid
the sound of chopping
is the winter pulse of this suburb.
At night, Desiree moves her chair
close to the fire
and talks on the phone
Dad rests his coffee on the grill
to keep it warm
while he goes out into the mist
for another log.
At midnight, alone, I open the fireplace door
and feed my poems on Annabel
to the flame.
The words dance with a heat and light
they never had on the page
each flicker warming my hands.
I go back to my room
to write some more food
for the fire burning
in this house.

*E*zra finds the hut

If you follow the bush track
    off Narrowneck Road for 500 metres
you'll see the ghost gum
    the one with the arrow
    pointing west
follow that track
    until you reach the bridge
before the creek
    there's an overgrown wallaby track
push through it
    until you see the tree
    with Jack & Annabel's initials.
Quiet now.
    look up at the ridge
    on the left
see the hut
    built by bushwalkers fifty years ago
if you go there after school
    you'll find Annabel & Jack
but hey,
    don't go there after school.

*M**egalong creek hut*

Ever since Desiree told me about this hut
I knew it would be the special place
    for Annabel and me
somewhere silent.
    her parents
my Dad
    even the ghost couldn't find us here.
we've cleaned it
    evicted the resident possum
nailed the walls and roof back
    the wind still creeps in
but we hold each other to keep warm
we take turns to tell stories
as the trees brush against the roof
and the world clouds over
    in the winter afternoon.
We've planned a night alone here
    but
neither of us has that much courage
one ghost is enough to handle.
    still
every afternoon with the thought of homework
and school fading
we run through the bush
to our special place
    and disappear
          from sight.

Annabel and the wild orchard

Sometimes I don't want to reach our hut
I want to take Jack's hand
follow the trail
 down to the six foot track
pick up a snake stick
 and like an old miner
follow that track to the valley
and there, with Jack,
 set up camp
pick apples from the wild orchard
 watch Jack try to build a fire
and when he's sweating with frustration
 offer him the matches
and laugh all through dinner
 and at night watch the stars
no higher than the cliff walls
and the two of us
holding tight for warmth
as sleep wraps around
 we dream in the soil
 of our days
 moist, firm, full
until the sun
 wakes
and offers us time
 to walk
 holding hands
in the wild orchard.

Making a Living

The funeral

We were twelve
the dead bird on the steps
Ezra touched the matted feathers
    with a stick
and wondered aloud
why it flew into a closed window.
We got Dad's shovel
buried it under the fir tree
lashed two sticks together
wrote RIP on the cross-stick
and stood looking at the grave
Ezra said he'd never seen
    anything dead before
I said I had
    and walked back to the house.

Desiree

Late at night
    when Jack and Dad are asleep
I stand naked in my bedroom
    in front of the mirror
I look at my breasts
    in the surgery fluorescent light
of my Mother's death
    I touch them
feel my nipples harden unwillingly
    it can kill me
this thing, this woman thing.
    I find a different lump every night
and lie awake
    wishing it away.
My last boyfriend tried to understand
    he even offered to inspect them for me
his hand made me forget, for a time
    but I know
it's not the cancer
    or the pain
it's the waiting
    as I pull the sweater
gently
    over my head.

Careers

It's Careers Advice Week
where a very serious man
    in a white shirt and thin black tie
talks to us, individually, about our futures.
With ten per cent unemployment
and all of us desperate to avoid
    thinking about next year
I don't like his chances.
When Ezra saw him yesterday
    he told the Advisor that his ambition
    was to never see his father again.
Now, knowing Ezra's father
    this seemed a worthy occupation
the Advisor handed Ezra a TAFE Handbook
    and made another appointment.
I've decided with my five minutes
    I'm going to talk non-stop
    and, hopefully, walk out.

I'm going to tell him
    I want to marry Annabel
    write a book of poems
        even people like him could read
    buy a house on a cliff
    find a cure for nose hair
    win a medal at the Poetry Olympics*
    be interviewed regularly on television
and never enter a school again
and never wear a white shirt with a thin black tie.

* POETRY OLYMPICS actually happen. The idea
    was originated in London by poet Michael Horowitz

*S*elling up

Last night
a Real Estate Agent visited.
Dad showed him the house
                    the view
        avoided the cubbyhouse
        promised to trim the hedge
they sat down and talked money
        and buyers moving west
        Interest Rates
        the chance of a quick sale
and all through the meeting
        Dad kept looking around
        as though somebody was watching him
until the Agent got worried
        left his card
        told Dad to "discuss it with the wife"

by then
        Desiree and I knew
we weren't selling
        because Mum
had already made her views
        hauntingly clear.

The wreck

last night
I dreamed I died.
A car accident
Ezra beside me
in the wreck
his teeth dripping with blood
we hung upside down
one breath away from the cliff edge
with the ghost gum holding our sway
and I touched Ezra
and shivered
I struggled to the door
and pushed
as the tree surrendered
we toppled
the car, Ezra, me
kept falling
until I landed
this morning.

*D*ad didn't come home last night

Dad didn't come home last night
me and the ghost waited
listened for the tyre crunch on the drive
for the drunken key in the lock
the ghost wasn't worried
she sat in front of her mirror
and looked at the family photos.
I lay in bed
    thinking of road accidents
    back street gangs
    police RBT units on the highway
then I remembered the woman
the one Dad refused to tell us about
    as he nervously straightened his tie
    and combed his hair (first time this week).

I thought I was the one
        supposed to be out all Saturday night
        not my fifty-year-old father!
why am I alone in bed
        with my sensible pyjamas
        and a good book?
why is Desiree snoring
        when our father's out on the town
        and we're home by midnight

and why, why is the ghost still smiling
        does she know something I don't …

Sunday lunch

Cold chicken, fresh bread
Dad and me on the veranda
Dad still in last night's clothes
we eat quietly
as he tells me
about his only big date in seven years.
The dinner, the wine
their children in every glass
and all the time
Dad's trying to flirt
until dessert
when he gives up and tells
this woman of his wife and her death
and the years drinking early evening
with his workmates
and coming home to us
and the photos on his dresser
and over coffee it takes hours
to tell a life story
and to listen to hers
and that's what they did all night
(a rueful smile over our chicken).
He talked all night, and listened.

he didn't mention his work
he talked like he's talking to me now
he talked until he knew
	the ghost still haunted him
	and always would.

This morning Dad came home
	to the photos on the dresser
and planned another big date
	seven years from today.

The earthquake

The earth moved last night
the ancient plates under our mountain shifted
    as windows spooked and rattled
    the lampshade cracked
and our wedding photo
    fell off the dresser.
Desiree slept
Jack snored
    I fastened the window
    turned off the lamp
    picked up the photo
and spent an hour holding the frame
    getting married all over again
while the earth
    threatened.

This morning
the papers reported
3.5 on the Richter Scale
and no damage
I didn't mention the wedding
but all morning I felt
the cruel aftershock.

What I do for a living

I spend my day in front of this ignorant computer
typing stories
no, not stories (stories have heart)
typing articles
on our trade deficit and unemployment figures
so people can read and worry over their cornflakes.
At lunch I cross Broadway
for a drink and a sandwich
forgetting my health deficit and waistline figures.
The other night Desiree asked me
why I wanted to be a journalist
and it took me exactly forty-nine minutes to
    think of an answer
and that was a simple "for the money"
because during forty-eight of those forty-nine
minutes
I remembered their childhood
    Jack's first day at school
    his little wave
    as the teacher lead him away
    and Desiree's laugh every morning
    at something on television
    and how it woke the house

and I realised I don't give a stuff
about politics, or inflation,
or rising interest rates,
as long as I keep hearing Desiree's laugh
and seeing Jack's pride
then I know what I really do
        for a living.

All her brain cells

I know why Desiree
        doesn't have a boyfriend
        and hasn't had one
        for a long time.
it's because
        she has perfect eyesight
        and all her brain cells.

Solo Desiree

Jack and Annabel have made love
I can tell
Jack doesn't bother me any more with questions
    on girls, or sex,
      or what he should do about his appearance.
He looks like one of those TV evangelists
    who've discovered God
    and the miracle of money
it's almost unbearable, his swagger,
    but at least
he doesn't brag out loud.
Annabel's OK too!
I spent the first hour after meeting her
    looking at her top lip
and I'm pleased to report
    there's a good trace of darkening hair
and thank Christ she doesn't giggle!
    or talk about music.

Even Dad liked her
> but I think he was just happy to see Jack
> bring a friend home
although he doesn't seem so pleased
when he meets my boyfriends
not that there's been anyone for a while
I'm going through my Nun stage
you know, wearing black
>> talking quietly
>> keeping my desires religiously confined
but not for much longer.
> If Jack and Annabel keep pawing each other
> when I'm watching television
I'm breaking my vows
> problem is,
men are easy to get rid of
> harder to find.

The ghost spoke to me last night

The ghost spoke to me last night
I was sleeping
I turned to the window where she sat
she whispered for me to tell Desiree
to stop looking into the mirror
and then she disappeared

the next morning
I told Desiree
she didn't believe me at first
then she gave me a kiss
went to her room
and came out in her favourite dress
and white stockings
she said she was having the day off
Dad smiled, and said he was too
they both looked at me, pleading
for me to jig school

this house is going mad.

*F*ather of the year

It's been a month since Dad had his big date
in that time he's devoted
every Saturday to Des and me
we've been out for lunch
       to the movies
         on a ferry cruise
and last week we camped the night
     in the Blue Gum Forest
Des and I are worried we'll never get rid of him!
He talks to me about Annabel
     and encourages Desiree to go out more
he tries to cook dinner
we have long involved talks
     on our life, our school, our future
it's like living with your Deputy Principal.

I've seen Dad in my room
    looking at my wall photos
he's started ironing Desiree's clothes
twice he's increased our allowance
he's talking of us going on holiday together
he said I could bring Annabel
and Desiree could bring anyone
    (Desiree looked ill)
he's stopped drinking wine with dinner
he cuts the fat off his meat
last week I saw him preparing to go jogging
I occasionally catch him looking at me as I read
    he looks satisfied
he gets home early from work
    and wants to play cricket with me in the backyard
he sits alone in the cubbyhouse
    staring across the valley
he says "nigh nigh" to us, as though we're
    children again.
Our Dad is going for father of the year
and slowly sending Desiree and me
completely mad.

Annabel writes a poem for english

I have been told by my English teacher
    she with the nervous twitch
    and perfect vowels
    stolen from British movies at the Savoy
that I should write a poem
    as an assignment
    and that the poem should be on NATURE,
    and I should make full use of
simile, metaphor, and alliteration.

Now, I like birds, and streams,
    and the odd tree as much as anyone
    but if I'm told to do something
    so bloody narrow again I'll
I'll
I'll

Nature
  (A poem with simile, metaphor, & alliteration)
the King Parrot
    drops like a stone
        like my Dad when he's drunk
        like a Nun's eyes before God

the King Parrot
    is stone
    is drunk
    is dead
dead door-nail dead darkly
definitely damn dead (oh dear!)

And as I hand this limp piece of protest
to my teacher
I see my English marks drop faster than
faster than
faster than a dead parrot!

*W*inter Annabel

I'm sick of people talking about
    this country as being only
    sun, beaches, and the outback.
Where I live it's cold, windy,
and the mist drops heavy in January.
While people fry on Bondi
I wear an overcoat and a wet nose
    and every house
    keeps a stack of firewood ready all summer.
Sure, it only snows a few times a year
but those winds punching through Megalong Valley
    make my teeth ache with cold
and I love it all!

I've never seen the sense
    in lying comatose on a pile of sand
    turning pink
    or swimming in each other's effluent
    that passes as surf.
And I like how the rail-thin *Dolly* victims
    in Year 11 desperately try to look slim
    in two jumpers and an overcoat.
My idea of fashion is a flannelette shirt
    and Levis in front of the fireplace.

People say the beach is the great equaliser
who are they kidding?
sit at Bondi and watch the boys flex
    and the girls walk bolt upright
    it looks like a nightmare episode of *Baywatch*.
The true equaliser is the mountain cold
    and stacks of clothes flung together
maybe then we'd listen to what each other is saying
    instead of checking out the best bods.

And as I wrap another layer
    around my Size 10
I think of Jack's favourite saying:
"today's tan is tomorrow's cancer".

I walk outside
and whistle at the wind.

Echoes

My son is seeing a girl

My son is seeing a girl
     and a ghost.
I hear him talking to Annabel
     in the chill afternoon
and I hear whispers
     to the ghost
in the long night.
I haven't told him I know.
What could I say?
In the past year
     he has grown tall
     his eyes sparkle the way of his mother's
and when he's reading
     I look at him with pride.

I know who the ghost is
I'm glad they talk
     I stare into the mirror
as the trees shadow through the window
     and I envy Jack.

I lean against the wall and listen.

He is talking to her
    a soft monologue
    that pumps through this house
    like an open vein.

I try to picture the ghost
    sitting at the edge of his bed
and the night grows suddenly dark
    and the whispers fade.

I return to bed
and wrap the blankets of memory
around me, tight.

Sex, sport, and nose hair
(according to Annabel)

Sex is what Jack and I practise at Megalong Creek.
Sex is my parents encouraging me to go out
    early Saturday night, so they can "talk".
Sex leers over my shoulder at the canteen.
Sex is the colour of the December bushfires
    with our hut feeling their hot breath.
Sex is what the school terms "personal development"
    as our parents look worried.

Sport is my Dad's idea of a Sunday out.
Sport is a short skirt in winter
    tossing a netball through the mist
    while our teacher sips coffee.
Sport does something to the brain of an everyday
male.
Sport rumbles down the stairs
    knocking Year 7s over
    as it swings its gorilla arms to the oval.

Nose Hair is what Jack thinks of more than me
Nose Hair tickles as we kiss
Nose Hair grows and grows and grows
Nose Hair is the forward brother of ear hair
Nose Hair longs to be plucked!

*B*lue mountains school

The clouds cover our school
as impenetrable as Science
         on a Friday afternoon
the black cockatoos crunch nuts
         and drop them from trees
like bombs cracking the schoolyard

Annabel and me on the seat
         our lips feeling their way
through the mist
when the Deputy Principal Mrs Jonestown
         like a tank
         comes lumbering through the murk
         guns blazing
         horn-rimmed glasses
         like heat-seeking missiles
aimed at Annabel and me

and she starts on with that
         "what sort of example is this to the
                  Juniors" stuff
and I try to defend with
         "no one can see us in this cloud"
but with the predictability of someone over thirty
         she shoots a "does that make it all right"

and now would not be the time
to mention love, peace,
and an end to the Cold War I fear
so we're marched back to class
prisoners of war
sentenced
to six months hard labour
and 2-Unit Maths
and the clouds come in thicker
soft cages
          hiding tanks clanking
around the perimeter fence
waiting ...

*B*loody rain

"Bloody rain" says Mr Chivers
bouncing a basketball
on the one dry patch of court
"bloody rain" he nods to our Sports class
and gives us the afternoon off.
Bloody rain all right
as Annabel and I run to Megalong Creek hut
faster than we ever have in Chivers's class
and the exercise we have in mind
we've been training for all year
but I doubt if old Chivers
will give us a medal if he ever finds out.
We high-jump into the hut
and strip down
climb under the blankets
and cheer the bloody rain
as it does a lap or two
around the mountain
while Annabel and me
embrace like winners should
          like good sports do
as Mr Chivers sips his third coffee
and twitches the bad knee
from his playing days

while miles away
Annabel and I
score a convincing victory
and for once in our school life
the words "Physical Education"
make sense ...

Confessions

"I like the back of your neck"

> her fingers roam
> untouched but hopefully washed territory
> I feel a twitch in my knee
> (of all places!)

"I like your ears"

> I've seen my Dad's ears grow big
> and old with him. The elephant
> with his memory in the mirror

"I like your mouth"

> but only when it's shut, or silent,
> keep it silent Jack
> the wet of our kiss soaks my insides

"I like your hair"

> my Dad again
> haircut like a McDonald's arch
> retreating to the safety of bald

"I like your eyes"

I look straight
think only of the Kurdish soldier
facing his firing squad
seeing beyond, and never looking back.

"I like your arms"

Annabel, give in. Just admit it
I'm your kind of guy
I'm perfect, OK.
What can you find to fault

"but about your nose hair, Jack ..."

The right reasons

I've been sitting here
trying to think of the one thing in my life
that will give it sense,
like they do in Hollywood movies
and after ninety minutes of formula
you get a happy family
with blonde children
and the wife always looks younger than she should
and the hero looks older
and the credits roll happily ever after
while Annabel and I walk along Narrowneck Road
knowing her parents are away
but I'm still thinking of this one thing
and all I get is

a nine-year-old boy
ducking wild plovers dive-bombing the schoolyard
thinking
     "what if they hit my eye"
or a twelve-year-old
riding beside the train tracks
looking for bits of human left
after the train smash
     "what if I find some skin
     what if I find some skin".

At fourteen, I'm standing in a pack of boys
waiting for the ball
so we can avoid bashing heads
and for once it comes my way
and I dive full-length to meet it
        "what if I meet someone's boot
        what if I meet someone's boot"
but I'm lucky, I score,
and no one has to mention fear for another week
or until now

when Annabel and I are in bed together
and I thought football and death
and blindness and parents and school
and alcohol and unlicensed cars
were scary
and you move one arm under my body
and your skin is not hard like
        the gloss of magazines
or cold like the railroad metal
or brittle like the beak of a dead plover

and I'm thinking as our bodies meet
that I'll remember this forever
and I just hope
it's for all the right reasons.

The bike ride

Annabel has the bottle
I carry maps and food
I'm scared of getting lost
she wants to cycle aimless
she pedals like a caged mouse
she checks her watch
she feels her pulse
she ties the knot of her hair
       tight against her neck
she smiles for me to lead
I strain to follow the curve of her road
I hear the birds chorus
       to witness such clatter
I am leaning over the handlebars
my shoes pull hard on the pedals
I breathe her scent with the headwind
She rests her thigh on the seat
       turns to wait for me
we ride double-file
we hold hands
       swing to keep balance

she tells me stories
I tell jokes
we suck water from the bottle as we ride
we stop
kiss with our mouths full
we blow water into each other's mouth
she smiles
I can feel the crease of her lips
We are in love with this bike ride.

*M*onday, the last before holidays

Monday, the last before holidays
Ezra and I walk to school
his plaster off, the skin still white
he tells me his father is moving out
later I watch him smile all through Maths.
Monday, the last before holidays
I see Annabel walk up to a bunch of guys
heckling this Year 8 girl
and punch the biggest guy
hard, cracking his smile
she walks away with the girl
and the school holds its breath
I write in my diary
never cross Annabel
never cross Annabel.
Monday, the last before holidays
rumour has it that
two Science teachers are to marry
and honeymoon at Surfers
this confirms our suspicions
that teachers like bank tellers
and public servants
in-breed with immunity.

Monday, the last before holidays
the Principal tells a joke during Assembly
and everyone laughs
not because it was funny
or his timing was right
or even that we understood it
but, after all,
it was
Monday, the last before holidays.

*M*s Curling

Ms Curling and I had a talk recently
not about my late essay
or laughing in class
or even my excuse for a uniform
we had a talk about sex
sex and AIDS
sex and babies
sex and Annabel
it was very interesting
watching my favourite teacher
tell me stuff I already knew
and squirm with embarrassment
Ms Curling looks very attractive
when embarrassed
particularly when I asked her about Annabel
how did she know?
was she taught this at University?
was there a subject called
     "STUDENTS HAVING SEX — how to find out"?
did she get top marks?
so we skipped Annabel
and discussed condoms
I said I liked orange ones
     and we ended our talk, in laughter.

Ms Curling and I sat together sometimes after that
I told her about the hut near Megalong Creek
             about my Dad not coming home
             about Desiree
Ms Curling said she'd like to meet my Dad
I said he was too old for her

I didn't know there were teachers like her
I thought the years of exposure to Year 9
dried them out,
made them brittle, hard.
she was OK
maybe I would let her meet my Dad ...
I'm sure the ghost would approve.

Annabel kisses

Annabel kisses like the wind whistling
through the wattle
Annabel kisses like a prayer I said
at the age of nine
I couldn't open my eyes for hours
Annabel kisses and our fireplace glows
Annabel kisses and the nuns at St Rita's
turn their heads
Annabel kisses as the dogs bark
Annabel kisses on October 6th
all afternoon
two days before my birthday
Annabel kisses and even the ghost is silent
Annabel kisses with red lipstick
and her hand softly
on my wrist
Annabel kisses and I think of toothpaste
the 1992 Grand Final
and the beach on a family holiday
Annabel kisses with her eyes open
Annabel kisses in her black dress
with silver buttons
Annabel kisses with a sharp intake
of breath
Annabel kisses me
Annabel kisses me
and I kiss back.

*I*t's easy

It's easy to tell your Mum
you're in love
with the guy from up the road
and that you and him
made love in your bed with the birthday sheets
when they were on holidays last weekend.
It's easy to ask for a second helping of guilt
and misplaced trust
as you share tea
with two spoons of tears
and a dash of broken promises.
It's easy to invite Jack for dinner
with the family
and feel his hand under the table
while you watch your Mum
reach for the carving knife
as Jack asks for a second helping.
It's easy to see the fear
in your Dad's eyes
as he struggles to make sense
of camping trips and story books
and Girl Guide meetings every Thursday
and his pride when I won the high jump
on his forty-fifth birthday
and tonight he looks at Jack
like he looks at his car when it won't start

it's easy
easy as kissing your childhood goodbye.

3 7 lines

She is the reason I walk home from school
    the long way
She talks all breath and throat
She keeps my picture on the wall
    next to a STOP sign
She says poetry books make good weapons
She says I look like a movie star
    I say Keanu Reeves
    she says, no, Roger Rabbit.
She listens to Madonna and Opera at the same time
She spoons sugar in her coffee
    but refuses to stir
She wears Egyptian sandals in summer
    I float down her Nile
She knocks at my door and shouts
    "Police. Open Up."

She wears black stockings with red flowers
She wears black stockings with Baxter boots
She wears black stockings
    I follow her step
She eats with a fork
    stays afraid of the knife
She kisses me in front of my Dad
    we all look out the window
She rides a bicycle like a threat
She says Maths teachers were born
    with glasses and bad haircuts
She likes Science
    but refuses to cut up the frog
She clenches her fist
    as we walk past McDonalds
She is waiting
    here
    now
She says love is like a shadow
    that scares you awake
She refuses to say more.

Telling the ghost

I'm going to tell the ghost to stay away
I don't know how I'm going to do it
but
I am going to
how long do you need a ghost for?
how long is Dad going to
    say I look like you
    carry your photo in his wallet
    mention you every night over dinner
I'll be seventeen in two weeks time
Annabel and I are having a private party
    in the hut
and then I'm coming home to Dad and Desiree, and
    dinner.
At midnight, I'm going to tell the ghost
    no more visits
it's not that I don't need her
    or want her to stay
I'm just too old to believe in it any more
seven years of talking to myself
seven years of listening
    and hearing a fading echo
    of a Mother I loved, and still do.

I'll just tell her straight
    blow a kiss
    smile (definitely won't cry)
and get on with this life.
I've decided it's time
I've got more than a memory
I see my Mother
    in my face
    in Desiree's hair, and her hands,
    in what we do in this world.
I know she'll understand
it's time
I definitely won't cry
at least
not until she's gone.

*E*choes

I woke early, dressed
climbed out the window
and sat on our roof
to watch the morning
I could hear the gang-gangs
welcoming the day
I knew I had a full hour
to sit here, and wait.
For the first time in my life
I'm waiting for NOTHING to happen.
I'm seventeen
I've cut my nose hair
     dressed in clothes my sister would approve of
I've washed the childhood from my eyes
I'm sitting on this roof
and I'm happy because all I can see
     are trees, the rising mist,
     the orange cliffs
     and our cubbyhouse, still standing.
I know in one hour my Dad will wake
     and cast his eyes to her photo
     and he'll know what his day lacks
     before he's had a chance to change it.

He needs his ghost
    whispering through the house
    arranging the days into sequence.
I climb down from the roof
    and walk around our yard.
I am alone
the only ghost I hear is the wind
I walk along Narrowneck Road
    past Annabel's house
    down to the Landslide Cliff
and for the last time
I shout the ghost's name
and turn
    without waiting for the echo.

821
HER

Herrick, Steven.

Love, ghosts & facial
hair.

21370

DATE			